THE LONGEST LETSGOBOY

THE LONGEST LETSGOBOY

WRITTEN BY **DERICK WILDER**

ILLUSTRATED BY **CÁTIA CHIEN**

chronicle books · san francisco

Mewmew wakes me,
rumbledrumming my tummy.

I strrrrretch my oldbones.

Fireball floats across brightblue,
playing hide-and-seek with puffers.
Swirlies ruffle the fur on my upsidedown.

SNIFF SNIFF
Oh boy, **oh boy, oh boy!**

Here comes Little,
my foreverfriend.

She gives me a happyface.
I wigglewag.

We shake and Little holds out a tastytreat,
letting me know I'm a gooddog,
oh yes I am.

Little calls out, "Letsgoboy!"
Her paws crunchcrunch across diggiedirt,
and waybacks fill my head.

I am an awwwpuppy again . . .
runjumping and tailchasing,
yipyapping constantly at branchjumpers,
leglifting endlessly on tallsticks.

Standing under those same tallsticks now,
Little still looks tiny. I want to runjump to her,
but am dogtired, so I must slowstep.

She waits, then we disappear
into bigwild.

I wuffwuff farewell to tweeters, branchjumpers, and fuzzhoppers,

then headdown to tallsticks,
colorfuls, and leafies,
never letting Little stray too far.

I hear tweeters' tender replies in my one good listener,
feel tallsticks' gentle trembles through diggiedirt.

They tell me that Little will always be welcome, always be safe.

We reach a bend in gurgleburble,
where hornheads and stripetails often visit,
and sipslurp cool sweetness.

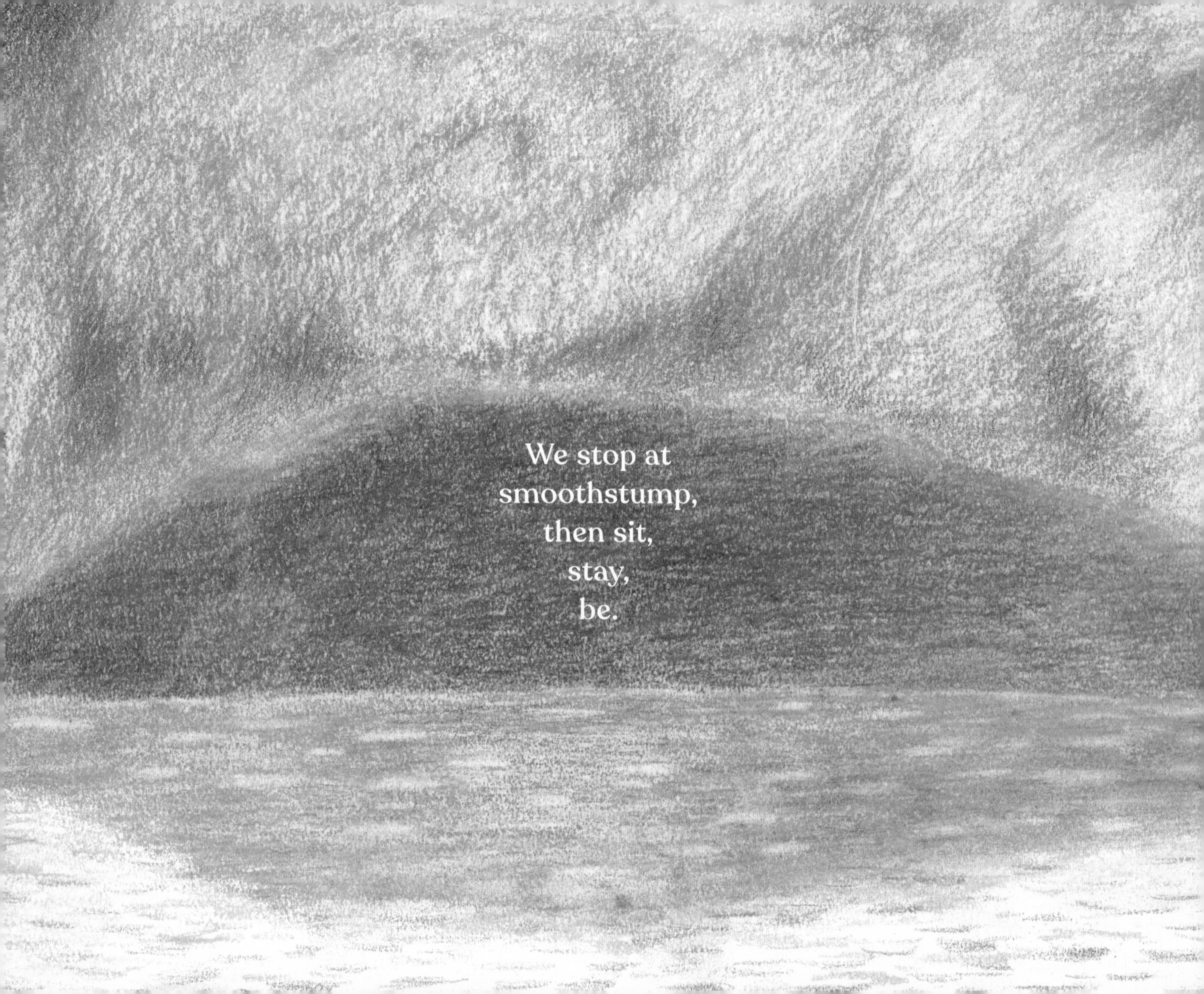

We stop at
smoothstump,
then sit,
stay,
be.

When shadows stretch out,

it is time to go.

Little gives me her tightest lovesqueeze.
I give her my wettest nosenuzzle.

I wait until Little is
inside, then slowstep to the
far corner of softgreen.

I circle once,
twice . . . then settle.

Mewmew's rough tongue
tickles my cheek.
She shares soothing rumbledrums,
letting me know I'm a gooddog,
oh yes I am.

Among peaceful tweetertunes
a distant "Letsgoboy!"
drifts down from puffers.

I take one last look at Little.
She will be okay,
and I am ready.

I close my eyes . . .

and feel the flutter
of beautifuls,
lifting me
above tallsticks.

My oldbones
feel new.

I can runjump again!

Little gathers with her pack of twopaws.
I miss them.
Dewdrops on their cheeks say they miss me, too.

Tallsticks lose
their fur,

then coldwhite covers bigwild
in a cozy blanket.

More lightdarks pass,
and coldwhite disappears.

Countless colorfuls
show their faces,
and new tweetertunes
bring joy to my listeners.

SNIFF SNIFF
Oh boy, **oh boy, oh boy!**
There goes Little.

She's on a letsgoboy when . . .

branchjumpers start scattering
and tallsticks begin grumbling.

And then I see him.
There, yipyapping constantly
and leglifting endlessly,
is an awwwpuppy.

Little gives him a lovesqueeze.
He gives her a slobberkiss.
Then he's off, runjumping and tailchasing.

Little gazes up at brightblue.
She gives me a happyface.
I wigglewag.

She is my foreverfriend.

For Taylor and Lakota,
my own Little and gooddog. –DW

For Raine Revere. –CC

Library of Congress Cataloging-in-Publication Data available.

ISBN 978-1-4521-7716-8

Manufactured in China.

Design by Lydia Ortiz.
Typeset in Recoleta.
The illustrations in this book were
rendered in mixed media.

10 9 8 7 6 5 4 3 2 1

Chronicle Books LLC
680 Second Street
San Francisco, California 94107

Chronicle Books—we see things differently.
Become part of our community at www.chroniclekids.com.